What Do Insects Do?

Susan Canizares • Pamela Chanko

Scholastic Inc.
New York • Toronto • London • Auckland • Sydney

Acknowledgments

Science Consultants: Patrick R. Thomas, Ph.D., Bronx Zoo/Wildlife Conservation Park; Glenn Phillips, The New York Botanical Garden; **Literacy Specialist:** Maria Utefsky Reading Recovery Coordinator, District 2, New York City

Design: MKR Design, Inc.

Photo Research: Barbara Scott

Endnotes: Susan Russell

———————————————

Photographs: Cover: Robert & Linda Mitchell; p. 1: Kenneth H. Thomas/Photo Researchers, Inc.; p. 2: C.A. Henley; p. 3: E.R. Degginger/Animals, Animals; p. 4: (l) Robert & Linda Mitchell; p. 4-5: Dwight Kuhn; p. 6: Gary Retherford/Photo Researchers, Inc.; p. 7: Hans Pfletschinger Peter Arnold, Inc.; p. 8: C.A. Henley; p. 9: Robert & Linda Mitchell; p. 10: C.A. Henley; p. 11 & 12: Robert & Linda Mitchell.

Library of Congress Cataloging-in-Publication Data
Canizares, Susan, 1960-
What do insects do? / Susan Canizares, Pamela Chanko.
p. cm. -- (Science emergent readers)
"Scholastic early childhood."
Includes index.
Summary: Photographs and simple text describe the many things that insects do.
ISBN 0-590-39794-X (pbk.: alk. paper)
1. Insects--Juvenile literature . [1. Insects.]
I. Chanko, Pamela, 1968-. II. Title. III. Series.
QL467.2.C35 1998
595.7--dc21   97-29197
CIP AC

20 19 18 17 16 15 14 13 12 11   03   02   01   00

What do insects do?

They jump.

They fly.

They eat.

They drink.

They cut.

They carry.

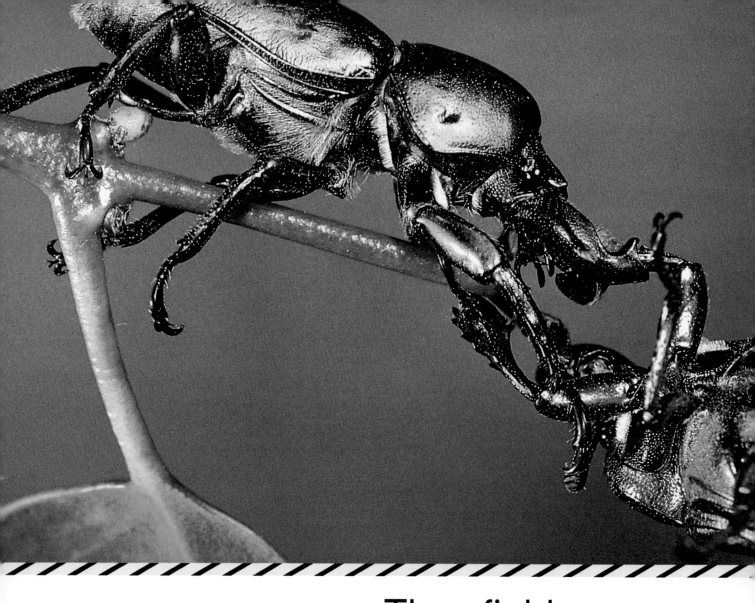

They fight.

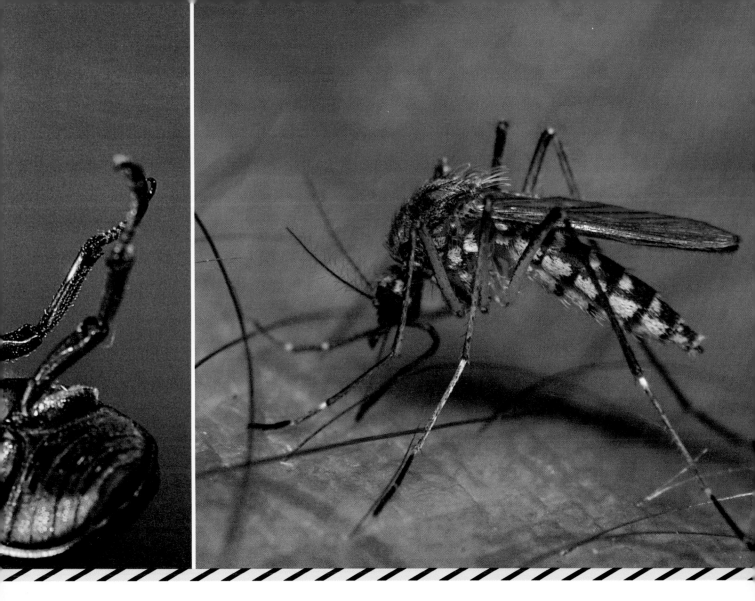

They bite.

They build.

They hide.

Insects look at you!

What Do Insects Do?

Insects do just what they need to do to survive. They are the most adaptable animals on the earth and have been here the longest. Insects find food and drink for themselves, build shelters, move around, hunt and escape, mate, and lay eggs for the next generation.

The fly (left) is in flight. Many insects have wings that enable them to go to where food can be found, to migrate to distant places, or to escape. The fly cruises at 5 mph. The grasshopper (right) is the best jumper in the insect world and can leap 36" or more.

Insects must nourish themselves. The Bird Grasshopper (left) is eating a blade of grass. The Praying Mantis (right) finds just one drop of water plenty to drink. Food for insects varies a great deal. Some insects feed on plants or sap and some eat other insects.

The Media Leafcutting Ant (left) cuts up leaves to bring back to the nest. It eats the fungus that grows on the leaves. Some ants in the community build the colony, while others guard it. The Red Ant (right) is about to help another ant carry the Inchworm back to the nest. Ants can carry up to 50 times their own weight.

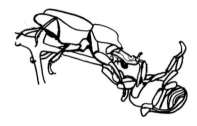

Although this Stag Beetle (left) looks quite ferocious, it is probably defending itself. The mosquito (right) gets nourishment from the blood of humans or animals. Its tiny mouth is specially designed for piercing and sucking, and can puncture the skin.

The Bull Ant (left) is one of the workers that is assigned the task of building. It is reconstructing the nest after a rain. The Leaf Grasshopper (right) protects itself from its enemies by camouflage. It is almost invisible on a leaf that is the same color and shape.

This Texas Shieldback Katydid seems to be looking at you! Katydids are known for the song they make in summer, which sounds like a shrill "katy-did-katy-didn't." Insects communicate with each other with touches, sounds, smells, and gestures.